THE LITTLE GREEN FROG

By

Beth Coombe Harris

SCHOOL OF TOMORROW®

Lewisville, Texas

ISBN 1-56265-012-2

4 5 6   Printing/Year   00 99

Printed in the United States of America

TABLE
OF
CONTENTS

CHAPTER 1

AMAH TELLS A STORY

"Come, my little lily flower. You must try to eat your dinner. See! I put molasses on your rice ball to make it nice."

"I don't want dinner," Biddy Forrester said with a sigh. "I don't want to eat. I'm too hot."

"I too feel the heat, and I do not like the noise of this great city," said Amah. Then she smiled. "I know what will help you feel better. Eat up your dinner, and I will tell you the story of how I got the little green frog." The Chinese lady's eyes became only little slits in her face as she laughed. Biddy was eating so fast that she almost knocked over her glass of milk!

Biddy always liked to hear a story, and her favorite story was the one about the little green frog. Oh, this was not a real frog. It was made of heavy, green stone and had two shiny little eyes set in its head. Amah sometimes gave it to Biddy to play with. On days like this, when it was too hot

1

to run and play outside, Biddy could pretend that the frog was really her pet, and she would play with it all day long.

Finally the last bit of rice ball was gone, and Biddy jumped up from the table. "I'm ready for the story, Amah." Together they sat on the woven mat on the floor, and Amah began her story.

"When I was very small, I lived in the rice fields with my own mother and father. One day a man came to our house. He was out of breath from running, and he was very much afraid. He begged my father to hide him from the men who chased him. This poor man's bare feet were all cut from the stones in the road. He had not eaten in a long time, and he was weak and tired. He could not tell my father what trouble had come to him, but only kept saying 'Hide me, hide me!' My father was a kind man and could not send the man away. He heard the men who were coming after the weak and tired one. Quickly Father took the man to an old well behind our house. There was no water in the well, so Father took off the boards that covered the hole and helped the man get into the well. Then Father put the boards back over him and sprinkled chicken feed on the boards.

"Just then the men arrived. They came into the house and looked all around, but the man was not there. They went into the shed behind the house, but the man was not there. They went right by the chickens who were eating the grain on the old well, and went away without finding the man."

Amah and Biddy laughed. "Your father was smart, Amah," Biddy said, laughing.

"Yes, he was very wise. And he was also kind. When the angry men had gone, he helped the man out of the well, took him to the house, and gave him food. He washed the man's feet and put medicine and bandages on them.

"The man stayed with us until he could walk again without pain. While he was there, he told us that he had been a priest in the temple in a village many miles away. He had argued with the other priests, and they tried to kill him. He was trying to get to his own village, where his family could protect him. Before he left us, he gave my father the little green frog. He told my father that it would bring happiness to the family. It was the only thing he had to give. He gave it because he was very grateful to my father for his kindness."

"Did the frog bring you happiness?" Biddy asked.

"No," answered Amah sadly. "Soon after that, my father died. Just before he died, he gave me the little frog and told me to take care of it. I made a little bag and put the frog inside. It seemed that the frog only brought us sadness, for we became very poor. Then a woman from the city told my mother that I would do as a wife for her son when he was older, and my mother thought that would be good, so I went to live with the woman in the city. She was unkind and made me work very hard. Because of this, I became sick and could not work. Then she did not want me and made me leave. I started to walk home, but I got worse on the way, for I had nothing to eat. And then, when I reached my home, my mother was not there. Another family now lived in our house."

"Poor Amah," Biddy said softly. "Where did your mother go?"

"I could not find her. The people would not let me stay, for they did not want to catch my sickness. They gave me a little food and then sent me away. Nobody wanted me. I did not know what to do or where to go. Finally I fell down by the side of the road and could not get up."

"Did you think you were going to die?"

"Yes, I did. But then I heard voices. They were not the voices of Chinese people; they were different. I opened my eyes, and I saw a man and woman with white faces looking at me. I had never seen such people, and I was so afraid that I screamed. Then they spoke to me, very kindly. 'Don't be afraid. We will take care of you,' they said. And who do you think was speaking so kindly to me?"

"I know! I know!" Biddy said quickly. "My mother and father."

"That's right. They took me to their home and took care of me until I was well. I had heard of the white missionaries, but I never knew they were so wonderful. Now I knew they were kind and good. They told me about the God in Heaven and about His Son, Jesus. I have been here since then, and the frog came with me, in the bag that I had made."

"God sent you here, didn't He? He sent you here to take care of me when Mommy and Daddy are busy."

"Yes, my little lily flower. That is why He sent me."

"Amah, did the frog ever bring you happiness? Did the frog make my parents find you on the road?"

"Oh no! It was God's goodness to me that brought them along the road where I was. I have learned not to trust in the frog, but to trust in God. Your mother says 'God has glad surprises.' "

"And what about your mother? Did she ever come home?"

"Your father helped me to find her. She had married again and did not want me, so I was glad to stay here."

"Thank you for the story," said Biddy as she got up from the mat. "Is it all right if I get the frog from the shelf in your room?"

Amah said it was all right, so Biddy got the frog and spent the rest of the day acting out the story that Amah had told her.

CHAPTER 2

GOODBYE TO CHINA

Dr. Forrester sat in the living room talking to his wife.

"Molly, I'm afraid that we will have to send Biddy back to England before long. She's been sick so much, and she can't seem to get well in this heat and in the city."

"I know you're right. But I don't want to send her so far away. Why, we won't be able to see her for a year—maybe two years at a time. And it takes weeks to send a letter to England! Dick, isn't there some way we can keep her here?"

"I don't really see how. Just think. When she goes back to England, she can have a good teacher, lots of room to play, healthy food, and clean air. We aren't sending her away forever."

"I know. But I'll miss her so much. And I don't even know your sister Hannah. She didn't seem to like children much when I saw her in England just before we left."

"It will be good for Hannah to have someone like Biddy around. Hannah will learn to be much kinder, I'm sure. I know she'll take good care of Biddy. And really, the only way that we could stay with Biddy is by going back to England too."

"Oh, we can't do that," said Mrs. Forrester quickly. She thought of all the sick Chinese people who came to their clinic for help. If the Forresters left, who would give them medicine, and who would tell them about the God who loved them? "No, I suppose the only thing to do is to send Biddy back to England. I hope she understands."

The next morning at breakfast, Biddy listened to her mother, her eyes wide with surprise. Mother was telling her about England, about Aunt Hannah, and about the long boat trip she would be taking to get to England.

"Aunt Hannah is eager to see you," Mrs. Forrester was saying, "and you will like England so much! You'll like the big yard to play in, and there are all kinds of flowers. You'll live out in the country, you won't have to listen to all the city noise, and it won't be so hot there in the summer. And you'll have lots of friends."

"I think I'd like to go," said Biddy, "but I want you and Daddy to come too."

"Well, Biddy, we would like to go with you, but you know that there won't be anyone to come and take over the clinic for two more years. Daddy and I have to stay here to help the people who come to the clinic."

"Then you come. Daddy is the doctor. He can stay."

"But if I go, Daddy will have to stay all alone. There is too much work for him to do by himself. He would have to spend all of his time just being a doctor and wouldn't have time to tell people about Jesus. You don't want to be selfish, do you? Would you rather keep your mommy all to yourself, or share me with the other people who need me?"

"I want you, Mommy!" Biddy cried. "Those Chinese don't need you. They can get someone else to help them!"

Just then a woman came running to the door. "Oh, come fast! My daughter spilled some boiling water on her foot. Come help!"

Dr. and Mrs. Forrester jumped up to help the girl, and Biddy went outside into the courtyard. At first she was angry, but then she began to feel ashamed. She walked along, kicking at the gravel on the ground. *What does Daddy think of me now?* she wondered. *He was glad when I was unselfish with my dolls and gave one to Hansan.* It made her sad to know that Daddy would be unhappy with her actions, but still she did not want to leave them here while she went to England. And then she thought, *I guess it makes Jesus unhappy too. I know He wouldn't want me to be so selfish.* She knew that Jesus loved her and that He knew about her problems, so she began to talk to Him.

"Lord Jesus, I know You don't want me to be selfish, but I do want my mommy and daddy. I guess I know what's right, but I don't want to do it. Please help me not to be so selfish. I am sorry that I am selfish. I don't want to be."

Just then her mother came back to the house. Biddy grabbed her hand and walked toward the house with her. "Mommy, I—I think I would like to go to England after all. And I think I'm big enough to go by myself."

Mrs. Forrester smiled and hugged Biddy. "I'm glad you decided to be unselfish. What made you decide?"

"Well, I know it doesn't make you and Daddy happy when I'm selfish, and I know it doesn't make Jesus happy. So I asked Jesus to help me do the right thing."

"You must remember that when Daddy and I are far away, Jesus will still be with you."

"I know," Biddy said.

"Come on, Biddy," said her mother. "Let's go find Amah and tell her the news."

When Amah heard, she began to cry. "My little lily flower, for you I am glad but for me, I cry. You will forget about me away off there."

"No I won't, Amah. I couldn't forget you. Please don't cry."

Amah tried to stop crying. "England is a good place, I think. There is much money there, and gold."

"Really? For everybody?"

"Oh, I think all are rich in England."

"I'll make a lot of money when I get there, and send it to Mommy and Daddy to build a hospital. There's no place for the sick people to stay. Then Daddy can do operations." She stopped. She would miss Amah. "I wish you could come with me and tell me stories, Amah."

Amah went to the shelf where the little green frog was kept. "Little lily flower," she said. "I would like to give you the frog to take with you—to keep always. It will make you think of Amah sometimes."

"Really, Amah? May I really have it?"

"Playing with it can give a small lily flower

happiness on dark days. You may have the frog."

Then it was time to start packing for the long trip to England. Biddy took along her Chinese clothes so that the boys and girls in England could see how the Chinese people dressed, and she took her Chinese books so that they could see the strange writing.

"I know you'll tell people about China, Biddy, but what else will you tell the people in England?" asked Mrs. Forrester.

"I'll tell them about the clinic," Biddy answered.

"And what else?"

"Oh! I'll tell them about Jesus, and how we teach the Chinese people about Him."

"I'm glad you will, Biddy. You know, people all over the world need to hear about Jesus—even the people in England."

Then Biddy laughed. "I'm going to be a missionary too, Mommy, a missionary to England."

When Mr. and Mrs. Broadbent came for Biddy two weeks later to take her to the boat with them, she was carrying the little green frog.

"Do you think that frog is worth anything, Dick?" Mrs. Forrester asked her husband.

"No, I think it's just soapstone. Besides, Amah gave it to Biddy as a keepsake."

Finally they all said goodbye, and Biddy Forrester began her long trip to England.

CHAPTER 3

A STRANGE COUNTRY AND
A NEW FRIEND

What an exciting trip Biddy had! First she and the Broadbents rode in a horse-drawn carriage. Then she noticed that as they got closer to the big cities on the coast of China, there were more and more people who were not Chinese. Ever since she had come to China several years ago, she and her parents had been the only English people she had known, and everyone had stared at them. Now no one even noticed her.

When they reached Hong Kong, they boarded a large boat. On the ship she found other children to play with on the long trip. Each time they came to a new port, they all ran to see the docks and the people who had come to meet the boat. They passed Singapore, Penang, Colombo, and Aden. Then they traveled up the Red Sea and on through the Suez Canal to Marseilles and Gibraltar and the Bay of Biscay. Biddy had never heard of those places, but she tried to find them on the map as they went along.

At last they came to the English Channel. They had been traveling for two months, and many of the people were tired and wanted to get off the boat. They began to shout and cheer when they saw England come into sight. Everyone hurried to finish packing and get ready for the customs officers, and at last the boat docked in England.

Biddy looked at the people who had come to meet their friends and relatives. She wished that her mommy and daddy were there to meet her, but they were far away in China. So she took Mrs. Broadbent's hand and held tightly as they got off the boat to meet Aunt Hannah.

Aunt Hannah was very tall and looked as if she never smiled. Mrs. Broadbent introduced Biddy to her aunt. Aunt Hannah said, "She looks like she's been sick."

"Well, I think she was sick in China, but she has gained weight since she left. Aren't you glad to be off the boat?" she asked Biddy.

"No," Biddy answered. "I had a good time."

"Just let her run wild for a while, Hannah," said Mrs. Broadbent. "I'm sure she'll be fine."

"Thank you, Sylvia, but I really don't want your advice. I think I know how to bring up a girl."

Biddy was feeling quite sure that Aunt Hannah really didn't know how to bring up a little girl. Mrs. Broadbent stooped to kiss Biddy goodbye and said that she would have to hurry to catch a train. Biddy almost asked to go with her, because she didn't think she was going to like her Aunt Hannah very much. But she remembered that she had told her mother she was big enough to go to England by herself. Now she would have to show Aunt Hannah that she was a big girl.

So she waved goodbye to Mrs. Broadbent as she and her husband went off in a taxi to the train. She could feel the tears in her eyes, and then they began to trickle down her cheeks.

Aunt Hannah placed a hand on Biddy's shoulder. "Now don't cry," she said. "If you are a good girl, I'm sure we will get along just fine. Let's go home now."

They rode in a taxi to Aunt Hannah's house, and by the time they got home, Biddy was all tired out. She could hardly climb the long staircase which led to the front door.

Aunt Hannah said, "I think you should go right to bed. You are awfully tired, and you have a little cold. I'll bring you tea in your room."

When Biddy had had her tea, Aunt Hannah came to rub some medicine on her chest to help get rid of her cold. "Mommy used to do this, too," she told Aunt Hannah. But it didn't feel quite the same, she thought to herself. When she had finished the rubbing, Aunt Hannah said, "Now you must try to go to sleep."

"But you haven't finished, Aunt Hannah," said Biddy.

"Oh? And what haven't I done, Bridget?"

"Mommy never puts me to bed without kissing me. And—and I like to be called Biddy, not Bridget."

Aunt Hannah kissed Biddy once on the cheek and left the room.

Biddy felt sad. I don't think she loves me very much, she thought. Once more she felt the tears coming to her eyes, but she didn't cry, and soon she fell asleep.

Next morning she went downstairs to eat breakfast with Aunt Hannah. "Are you going visiting this morning, Aunt Hannah?"

"Visiting? Why no! I hardly ever go visiting, and never in the morning."

"Oh. Well, do you work in a clinic or a hospital or something in the mornings?"

"No. Remember, you're in England now. I'm not a missionary like your parents. When people get sick, they pay for a doctor to come to their house or they go to his office or they go to a hospital."

"But you tell people about Jesus, don't you?" Biddy asked.

"Bridget, you ask too many questions. Little girls should be seen and not heard. It's very impolite to ask people such personal questions."

Biddy began to smile. "Mommy said that was what they used to tell her. She didn't think anybody said it nowadays!"

"I don't care what your mother said, that is what I believe," Aunt Hannah said sternly.

So Biddy became quiet and finished her breakfast. When she had finished, she started outside to play.

"Put on your coat," said Aunt Hannah.

"Oh, it's warm," said Biddy, going toward the door. "I don't need a coat."

Aunt Hannah stood up quickly from the table. "Bridget, when I tell you to do something, I expect you to do it and not to argue with me. Now put on your coat. I don't want you to catch another cold."

"All right," said Biddy quietly, and went upstairs to get her coat. When she came down, she carried the little green frog.

"What in the world is that?" said Aunt Hannah.

"It's mine. Amah gave it to me," answered Biddy, afraid that Aunt Hannah would think she had taken it without permission.

"Strange toy for a little girl," was all Aunt Hannah said, and Biddy went out into the yard, or garden, as it is called in England.

"Froggy," she said. "This is England. Just look at it! I wonder if we'll find any gold, like Amah said."

She walked around the yard, sniffing the flowers and looking closely at the clover. Then she began to feel lonely. There was no one around—no other children, no busy city streets, not even Amah, who had always been with her. The more she thought about China, the more she wanted to go back. She missed the Chinese people, and she missed her mommy and daddy. She sat down beside a bush with Froggy in her lap and started to cry. But then she was afraid that Aunt Hannah might come out and find her crying and wouldn't like it, so she tried to stop.

"Froggy," she said, "England is a nice place. We can come outside all alone. And look at this garden. It's beautiful. This is much better than China, isn't it?" She made Froggy nod yes. She got up, and then she saw some big white flowers that she hadn't seen before. She started to smell one of them, but there was a bee inside the flower! Biddy jumped back and the bee buzzed around her head for a minute, then flew away.

I'd like to pick some, thought Biddy, but I can't because they aren't mine. Oh well. I can smell them, now that the bee's gone.

She walked along smelling of each different flower, getting yellow pollen all over her nose and cheeks. She walked all around the garden, through the gate, and down the road, sniffing the flowers.

Finally she came to the village church. Behind the church was a cemetery with lots of small trees and many flowers. She had never seen a cemetery like this in China, and she didn't know what it was.

"What a funny garden," she said. "I think I'll go in." She tried to push the gate open, but it was too big and heavy. Just then an old man came along with a shovel in his hand, and he opened the gate. Biddy said good morning and followed him inside. "Does this funny garden belong to you?" she asked.

The old man looked surprised, then took off his hat and scratched his head. He smiled and said, "No, little miss. This doesn't belong to me. Some folks call it God's acre. I suppose, come to think of it, it could be called God's garden."

"Listen, miss," he said, "I'm going to be busy now. You go and play." Then he saw that Biddy was unhappy. "I'll tell you what. You go and see my missus. She lives down in that little house." He pointed to a small white house near the gate.

Biddy ran off down the road toward the house. "This is just like China," she said to Froggy. "I'm going visiting just like Mommy."

When she came to the door, an old woman was sitting at the kitchen table peeling potatoes. The door was wide open, but Biddy knocked anyway.

The old woman looked up. "Why, say, aren't you the little girl that's come from China to live with Miss Forrester?"

"Yes, ma'am," answered Biddy.

"Come right in. Why, I knew your father when he was a little boy. How nice of you to come and see me."

Biddy came in and looked around the kitchen. It was all so different from China!

The woman was talking to her. "How is it you've come so far without your mother and father?"

"Oh, they have lots of work to do in China. They can't leave until some other missionaries come to take over the clinic. So I came by myself, so I could get well, and so I could get lots of money."

"Money? What for?"

"Daddy wants it to build a hospital. I'm going to send it to him when I get some. There are lots of sick people there, and they can't all be helped 'cause there's only a clinic, not a real hospital. Besides, if they can stay in a hospital, we have more time to tell them about Jesus. Do you know about Jesus?"

"Yes, I do. Everyone here knows about Jesus. We aren't heathen, like the Chinese."

"Well, that's good. Do you love Him, like Mommy and Daddy and I do?"

The woman didn't want to tell Biddy that she used to love Jesus very much, a long time ago, but that now she didn't think about Him at all. She said, "I wonder if you know any little girls who like cookies. I've just baked some and I'm going to get them out of the oven right now."

"I like cookies!" exclaimed Biddy.

The woman laughed. "I thought so. Say! I don't even know what your first name is. What is it?"

"My name's Bridget, but I like to be called Biddy. What's your name?"

"I am Mrs. Camp. We'll pour a glass of milk while the cookies cool off a bit."

So Biddy ate all the cookies she wanted as she sat in Mrs. Camp's strange English kitchen and talked with her new friend.

CHAPTER 4

A PLAYMATE FOR BIDDY

Biddy swallowed the last bite of her last cookie. "I think I'd better go now," she said. "I'd like to come and visit some other time, if that's all right. When I come again, I'll tell you a story."

"Come whenever you want to," said Mrs. Camp. "Do you get nice things like cookies and milk and butter in China?"

"We were in the part of China where it was awful hot, so the butter was always melted, but—but I like China." Then she said sadly, "That's where Daddy and Mommy live."

"Well, don't you worry. They'll come home before long. You'll soon find lots of nice people here. Come again soon. I'd like to hear your story."

Biddy left the kitchen and turned to wave goodbye to Mrs. Camp, who called once more, "Come again." Biddy went out the gate, then stood for a moment, wondering what to do next. She saw a gate standing open and a path that led into the field down the road, so she decided to go exploring. As she followed the path, she found a small pond with ducks swimming on it. She quickly hunted through her pockets and found some crumbs of bread and threw them to the ducks. How funny they looked standing on their heads in the water as they went after the crumbs! Biddy laughed as she threw in the last bit of bread. Suddenly she heard someone say "Hello!" Biddy turned around and saw a boy a little bigger than she was.

"Hello," she said. "What's your name?"

"I'm Jock. I never saw you before. Where did you come from?"

"I came from China yesterday."

"You couldn't come from China in a day. It's a long ways off."

"I mean I finished coming yesterday. Where did you come from?" Biddy asked.

"I came from Scotland. I'm staying at the farm over there, 'cause I've been sick. I was so sick I nearly died," he said proudly.

"I could have died in China, if I'd wanted to. I was sick lots of times."

"Well, you're here anyway. Let's play. What's your name?"

"It's Biddy. Let's play Giants."

"Giants? What kind of game is that?"

"You know," said Biddy. "Giants. I'll be David and you be Goliath."

"Who's that?" said Jock with a frown.

"Don't you know that story? It's in the Bible."

"I don't know what's in the Bible."

"Oh. Well, I'll tell you the story then. Once a long time ago, there was a boy called David. He kept sheep."

"We have lots of sheep in Scotland. Was David a farm boy?" asked Jock.

"Sort of. He was a shepherd, and a bear came one day and tried to get the sheep, and he killed it. And one day a lion came, and he killed it too. He killed both of them bare-handed."

"I guess he didn't live in Scotland. No bears and lions around there."

"No, his country was far away. It wasn't China either. But anyway—"

Jock interrupted. "I don't think a boy could kill a bear and a lion by himself."

Biddy sighed. "Don't you know? David trusted God to help him. 'Course nobody could do it by himself. But God helped him. One day when David's country was having a war, a big giant came down on the field. His name was Goliath and he was so big that none of David's people would go and fight him. Now David's brothers were at the battle, and his father sent him with some lunch for them—some cheese and some other good things—"

"I wish he'd come along right now," said Jock. "I'd like something to eat."

"Are you greedy?"

"No, but I'm hungry. I had some Cornflakes this morning. And an egg. And three pieces of toast with butter and jelly. But I'm hungry again."

"I just had a bunch of cookies over at Mrs. Camp's, so I'm not hungry. She lives by God's garden."

"God's garden! Where's that?"

"Just down the road, inside that gate."

"Ha, ha! You're funny! That's a cemetery, where they bury people when they're dead."

"Well, you can call it that if you like, but it is God's garden. The man who takes care of it told me so. And if they put people there when they die, it really is God's garden. 'Cause if they love Him, then they go to be with Him in Heaven. So there."

"I don't know anything about that, but I guess it doesn't matter. What's that thing you're carrying?"

"This is Froggy." She held him up for Jock to see. "I brought him from China. You can hold him if you want."

Jock took the heavy frog. "Hmm. Nice frog. Say," he said, as he handed Froggy to Biddy, "are you going to finish that giant story?"

"Oh! I almost forgot. David got to the battle and saw that everyone was afraid to fight the giant, so he said, 'I'll go and fight him. I'm not afraid.' "

"He really thought he was important, didn't he?"

"No, he just knew that God would help him. He had already killed a lion and a bear because God helped him, so why not a giant? The king wanted David to get all dressed up in armor and take a sword, but David didn't do that. The only way he knew how to fight was with his slingshot. So he went down in that field and called Goliath, and Goliath just laughed at him. David picked up five stones from beside a little stream, put one in his sling, shot it, and it hit Goliath right in the head and he fell down dead."

"Hooray!" shouted Jock. "That's a good story. Is it really true?"

"Certainly it's true."

"He was a good shot. It was a good thing that stone killed the giant the first time, or the giant would have got David."

"But you forgot. God helped David. He couldn't lose."

Jock looked puzzled. "I don't know too much about God, but that's a good story anyway. Well, let's play! I'll be David, and you can be Goliath."

"No," said Biddy. "You're bigger. You be Goliath."

"Well, all right, but don't you hit me with any stones."

"I'll only pretend."

"Say, I know what we could do. There's a baby girl at the farm, and she's got a real soft ball that she plays with. I could bring that tomorrow, and you could hit me with it and it wouldn't hurt at all."

"That'll be fun. But I haven't finished all the story yet, the part about the giants we fight today."

"There aren't any giants around here."

"Yes there are. There's Giant Selfishness, like I had to fight when I wanted to keep Mommy and Daddy all to myself instead of letting them help the people in China. There's Giant Temper and Giant Mischief and—"

Biddy stopped suddenly. "Look, Jock! That duck looks like he's gotten his head caught on the bottom. He'll drown for sure."

She ran toward the pond. The ground looked solid, but it was only a thin crust that had dried in the sun. Underneath there was thick, black mud. Biddy ran to the edge of the water, and before she could get away, her feet were ankle-deep in the mud. "Oh!" she cried as she tried to pull her feet free. Each step made them muddier and muddier.

"Here," called Jock. "I'll give you a hand."

He helped to pull her out of the mud, then said, "Give me your shoes and socks. I'll wash them off in the pond. And look— there goes that duck. He wasn't caught after all!"

Just then they heard a sharp whistle. "That means I have to go," said Jock sadly. "I guess I can't help you. I promised my mother I'd always come when Mrs. Brown called me. You sure are a mess. Will they punish you?"

"I don't know. I just came yesterday, and this is the first naughty thing I've done."

"Well, it wasn't exactly naughty. It was an accident. Tell them that. Who do you stay with?"

"With Miss Hannah Forrester, my aunt. But she has a lady named Maria who helps her. They're both old, so I don't suppose they will understand an accident. I'll have to fight Giant Fear and go an 'fess. I'll have to be brave and grownup."

"I'm sorry I can't come with you, but I have to run. Goodbye. See you tomorrow."

Jock ran off to the farm up the road, and Biddy slowly walked home. The mud in her shoes felt terrible, and her feet began to get sore as the shoes slipped up and down on her heels. The closer she got to home, the more afraid she was.

She was nearly home when she met Maria coming out to the road. "Where have you been?" asked Maria. "Hannah is out, and she told me you were playing in the garden. I've been hunting everywhere for you. You're a naughty girl." Then she saw Biddy's feet. "My patience, child! What have you been doing?"

"I'm sorry. I walked in some mud. I didn't know it was there. It was an accident," Biddy said, as the tears came to her eyes.

"I should think you were big enough to see where you were going. A fine mess you're in. I guess I'll always be having this sort of thing to clean up now that you're here."

"I'm sorry," said Biddy, trying not to cry. "But I had to come here, even if I didn't want to."

Maria was sorry that she had been angry. "Well, we won't say any more about it. Come on. We'd better get you cleaned up before your aunt gets home."

So Maria washed Biddy's feet, put clean shoes and socks on her, and fixed a good lunch of soup and crackers, with pudding and whipped cream for dessert.

CHAPTER 5

FUN IN THE KITCHEN

Biddy talked cheerfully to Aunt Hannah at teatime that day.

"Did you have a good day, Aunt Hannah?" she asked.

"The usual, Bridget," she answered.

"Were people glad to hear about Jesus, or did they get mad at you?"

Aunt Hannah looked surprised. "Bridget, you must remember that you aren't in China. We don't go into people's houses talking about religion here. Your father and mother are missionaries, and it is their work to do that sort of thing. Would you like some of this sponge cake? Maria made it specially for you."

"Really? That was nice of her."

"And what did you do this morning?" asked Aunt Hannah.

"Well, first I went to God's garden, and a man there said I could visit his wife, so I did, and she gave me cookies and milk. She said I could go to see her again. Then I met a heathen—"

"A heathen! What are you talking about?"

"Well, he said he didn't know about the Bible or about God, so he's a heathen. That's what my father said. Anyway, I'm going to teach him."

"I suppose you mean Jock, from the farm up the road. You two should just play and not talk about such things as religion."

"But Jock doesn't even know that God loves him. Everyone should know that."

When she thought about Jock, she thought about fighting giants. And then she remembered her muddy shoes. She wondered if Maria had told Aunt Hannah about the accident yet.

I must fight Giant Fear, she thought. But that wasn't easy. Aunt Hannah might punish her. She didn't look very kind. But finally she said, very softly, "Aunt Hannah, I have to tell you something."

Aunt Hannah didn't encourage her to say more. She just looked at her and waited.

"I didn't mean to. It looked like dry ground, but it was all sticky."

"Tell me plainly what you did, Bridget," Aunt Hannah said.

"It was down by the pond. I thought a duck was drowning, and I ran to see if I could help him, and my feet went down in the mud. I—I guess I ruined my shoes. Maria washed them off."

When Aunt Hannah did not say anything, Biddy asked, "Are you very angry?"

"No," said Aunt Hannah. "I won't be angry with you unless you are disobedient or if you don't tell the truth. I hope you will be more careful, though. It's all right if you play outside with Jock. Now finish your tea and don't talk any more."

"Thank you," Biddy said, very glad that she would not be punished.

Next morning, when breakfast was over, Biddy was just going to get her coat and go out when Aunt Hannah stopped her.

"It's raining, Bridget. Sit down and play quietly with your doll. I have letters to write and cannot be disturbed."

Biddy sighed. She didn't much like playing inside. First she played with Froggy, pretending that they were back in China and that Amah was telling the story of how Froggy came to be hers. But that made her homesick for China, and the quiet room seemed even quieter without Amah to talk to. So she played with her doll, putting her to bed on the sofa, pretending that dolly was sick and she was the nurse. Then she counted raindrops for a while. She thought it would be fun to go out and wade in the puddles. After all, Aunt Hannah didn't really say she couldn't go out. I'll go upstairs and get my coat. I could borrow Aunt Hannah's big umbrella, she thought.

But inside a little voice kept whispering, "You know you shouldn't do it. You should fight Giant Disobedience."

So Biddy asked Jesus to help her to be happy inside. Just then the door opened, and Maria peeked in. "There you are. I've been looking for you to come and help me in the kitchen."

"What are you doing?" Biddy asked, glad for something to do.

"Making pies."

Then Biddy was very happy. "I'd be glad to help. We are going to be good friends, aren't we?"

"Of course we are. I've got a bit of a temper, but you shouldn't take any notice of that."

"Do you fight Giant Temper?"

"Yes, I suppose I do," said Maria, as she tied a big apron around Biddy. "But I don't always win."

So Biddy spent the morning rolling out pieces of pastry and covering them with sugar and raisins, and then baking them in the oven.

At lunchtime, they ate some of the little pies. Aunt Hannah said, "Tomorrow we'll go downtown and buy you a pair of rubber boots. Then when the grass is damp, you can still go out."

"Oh, thank you!" Biddy said. Then she added, "Are you sure you can afford it?"

Aunt Hannah smiled. "Yes, I can afford it."

"You look nice when you smile," Biddy said.

The smile left Aunt Hannah's face. "It's rude to make personal remarks," she said.

Biddy wondered what "personal remarks" were, but she finished her lunch without asking.

Biddy was very excited about her trip downtown. Everything was new and strange to her. First they bought a raincoat and boots, and then they went to a shop where Biddy had ice cream for the very first time in her life. She was so happy that she skipped down the sidewalk.

When they got home, she said, "Thank you, Aunt Hannah. We had a good time, didn't we?"

And again Aunt Hannah smiled.

CHAPTER 6

VISITING THE CAMPS

For two days the weather was stormy. Biddy could not go outside at all. Aunt Hannah gave her an apron to hem. Biddy thought it wasn't much fun to sew, but she tried, and after a long time she finished the hem.

Aunt Hannah looked at it carefully, then shook her head. "When I was your age, I could put in a much neater hem that that. I think you need more practice. From now on you should sew for a half hour each day. When you can sew better, then I'll teach you how to knit. Now I'm going to write to your father and mother. Would you like to send a message to them?"

"Yes. Tell Mommy that in England little girls sew and sew and sew until their fingers fall off!"

"Why, Biddy! You must learn to sew. All girls do. It will be good for you. Don't you have a nicer message than that to send to China?"

"I can write a letter myself. May I write one and send it with yours?"

"You can write one. If it's neat, I'll send it."

"Mommy won't mind if it isn't too neat, if I try hard. She'll say, 'Biddy did her best.' "

"Don't argue, Biddy. You certainly like to tell your own opinions."

Aunt Hannah gave her a pencil and a piece of paper, and Biddy sat down to write to her parents. She wrote very carefully, asking Aunt Hannah how to spell the hard words.

Dear Daddy and Mommy,

I wish you were here. I love you lots. A nice lady gave me cookies. Ant Hana got me some boots and a raincoat. I am learning to so. I hemmed a apron, and my hand hurts. Love and kisses good-bye,

From Biddy

She took the letter to Aunt Hannah, who said she would send it. She frowned at the letter. "You missed the easy words and spelled the hard words right."

"That's because I asked you how to spell the hard ones," Biddy said with a grin.

Finally the rain stopped. Biddy ran outside to play. She found Jock standing just outside the gate.

"Where have you been lately?" he asked. "I've been looking for you every day."

"Aunt Hannah wouldn't let me go out in the rain. What shall we do?"

"Can you play cricket?" Jock asked.

"No."

"Can you play marbles?"

"No."

Jock looked around for something else to do. "I guess it's because you're a girl that you can't do anything," Jock said sadly.

"Well, can you sew?" Biddy asked.

"No."

"Can you speak Chinese?"

"No."

"I guess it's cause you're a boy that you can't do anything," she said, laughing.

Jock chased her down the road. When they were out of breath they stopped. "Can you really speak Chinese?" Jock asked.

"Certainly I can," said Biddy, and began to say a poem in Chinese.

"What was that?" asked Jock.

"It's a poem that Amah taught me. It's about a worm that wanted to be a bird."

"Say some more. It's funny."

The children were so interested in Chinese that they didn't notice an elderly man standing in the road listening to them.

After a while he said, "Excuse me, children. I've been listening to you for a few minutes here. Has the little girl come from China?"

"Yes, sir. I came two weeks ago."

"Well, how interesting. I lived in China for many years. It is quite nice to hear someone speak Chinese. You must come and see me someday, and we'll talk Chinese together. Where are you living?"

"With Aunt Hannah at Dale House," Biddy said.

"And what is your Aunt Hannah's last name?"

"Forrester. The same as mine."

"Well, Miss Forrester and I are friends. Right now I have some errands to do, but I'll certainly have to see Miss Forrester and ask her to allow you to come and visit me. Goodbye now." He waved as he walked off down the road.

"I wonder where he lives," Biddy said.

"I know. He lives in a big house called the Grange. His name is Mr. Digby, and he's very rich. I heard Mr. Brown talking about him," Jock told her. "When he asks you to come, see if I can come too."

"Well, I don't know," Biddy said teasing Jock. "Since you don't speak Chinese—but I'll tell him you're a nice boy."

That made Jock feel better. "What shall we do now?" he asked.

"First we'll go and see Mrs. Camp. I told her I'd come and visit. Then we'll play Giants."

"Oh, yes! I remembered the ball." He pulled it from his jacket pocket.

Biddy reached into her own pocket. "I've got Froggy with me. I thought Mrs. Camp would like to see something from China and hear about how Amah got him."

"He's as big as a real frog. I like him," Jock said.

"He's nice and cool and smooth."

Jock touched the frog, then drew back quickly. "He is cool and smooth—almost like a real frog!"

Biddy put Froggy in her pocket, and she and Jock had a race to Mrs. Camp's house. They found Mr. Camp sitting by the fire instead of being at work in the cemetery. After they had said hello and Biddy introduced her friend, she asked, "Why aren't you working today, Mr. Camp?"

"I've got rheumatism, missy. It hurts my leg when the weather is rainy."

Biddy looked sad. "That's too bad. Can't you go and get medicine for it?"

"Yes, I've got some medicine already. It should be better soon."

"We'd better pray and ask God to make it better. Or have you prayed already?"

"Well, no, I don't pray much, missy." Mr. Camp smiled. "I don't know that God really hears prayer anyway."

"Of course He does!" Biddy exclaimed.

"Ah, but does He answer prayer?"

"Oh, yes, He's answered every one I ever prayed. And Mommy's and Daddy's too. Only sometimes He says no, and that's His answer."

"Well, I guess I never thought of that," Mrs. Camp said, looking thoughtful.

Mrs. Camp said, "Where's that story you were going to tell me?"

"Shall I tell you the giant story?"

"No," said Jock. "I heard that one the other day."

"I know another one about a giant."

Mrs. Camp said, "I know David and Goliath, but that's the only one. Which one do you know?"

Jock interrupted again. "I know Jack and the Beanstalk. That's a giant story."

"I don't know that one. Let me tell the one I know."

So Biddy began. "When David was old, he met another giant one day. He had a funny name, something about Ish."

"What a silly name," said Jock, laughing.

"That's all right," said Mrs. Camp. "Go on with your story."

"This is a sad story, because when David met this giant, he couldn't fight. David's nephew came just in time and killed the giant, so David was saved."

"Wait! I thought you said the other day that David killed Goliath because God helped him. Why didn't God help him kill this one?"

"Well, you see, God did it to show David that he should have stayed home where he belonged. God helped the nephew to kill the giant."

"Well," said Mr. Camp, "I'm glad there aren't any giants today. With my rheumatism, I guess I wouldn't be much good at fightin'."

"Oh, we have lots of giants! Maria fights Giant Temper and I fight Giant Disobedience, and there's Giant Selfishness—"

"Say," Jock said loudly, "I don't suppose you've been baking cookies this morning, have you, Mrs. Camp?"

Mrs. Camp laughed. "As a matter of fact, I haven't, but I do have some gingerbread. Would that do?"

"Oh, thank you," Jock answered, and soon he and Biddy were each enjoying a piece of gingerbread.

When they left the house, Biddy scolded Jock. "You shouldn't say things like that. It was just like asking, and that's not good manners."

"Oh, it doesn't matter," said Jock. "If I hadn't asked, we might not have got any."

"Well, you should have waited till Mrs. Camp offered. Oh, well, let's play Giants."

CHAPTER 7

PLUMS FOR SALE

One hot morning Jock and Biddy were sitting in the shade of an oak tree.

"Tell me where you got that frog," Jock said.

So Biddy told him the story that Amah had told her, all about the man who ran away from the temple priests and gave the frog as thanks for Amah's father's kindness.

"Did those people think Froggy was worth a lot of money or something?" asked Jock.

"Maybe. Maybe they even worshiped Froggy like a god. In China they do that."

"Tell me about China."

"Well, Chinese people have yellow skins and narrow eyes, and lots of people there can't read or write. They wear coats with big sleeves. And they eat rice and lots of vegetables, but not too much meat. And they are sick a lot."

"That's why your mother and father are there."

"That's right. Only they need a hospital. All there is in our city is a clinic, and people can't stay there till they're well." Then Biddy remembered what her Amah had told her. *There's lots of money in England.*

"Jock," she asked thoughtfully, "where do you get money in England? Amah said everyone was rich, and you could get all the money you wanted. But I haven't seen any and don't know how to get it."

"Didn't you ever make any money before? Or get an allowance?"

"No, my parents got money in the mail. I couldn't go in the stores in China, and I guess I never wondered about it before."

"Well, here's how you get money," Jock began. "You find a job, do some work for somebody, and they pay you money."

"Who could I work for? What could I do? I want to make some money so I can send it to my parents and they can use it to buy a hospital."

Jock thought for a moment. "Say, I know what we could do. Mr. Brown said this morning that he's got too many plums on his trees, and I could have all I want. We could pick the plums and sell them to people and you can have the money."

Biddy jumped up excitedly. "Oh, let's go right now!"

So off they went to Mr. Brown's farm. They got two large baskets from Mrs. Brown and went to the orchard to pick plums.

The day grew hotter and the baskets got heavier, but the two children kept at their work. Soon the baskets were filled, and Jock and Biddy started out to sell them in town.

Jock went to the first house, and sold some of the plums. When Biddy went to the next house, the lady who came to the door did not want any, and Biddy was sad. But at the next house, the maid came to the door and was glad to see the plums for sale. She bought two pounds.

Jock had sold some more plums, and it seemed that they were having a good day. They went on down the street, and Biddy did not notice that Aunt Hannah was sitting on the front porch of a house across the street.

The lady sitting with Aunt Hannah said, "Look at those children. I wonder what they are doing."

Aunt Hannah was very surprised to see Biddy and Jock, but all she said to her friend was "I suppose they are playing some kind of game."

At last the plums were all sold, and Jock and Biddy started for home. They were tired and hungry and dirty, but they had made two dollars and seventy-three cents. Jock gave it all to Biddy and went home to get his supper.

Biddy came into the house with a smile on her face. "Look!" she cried as soon as she saw Aunt Hannah, and held out the money for her to see.

But Aunt Hannah didn't look at the money. She looked at Biddy's dirty dress. "Go and wash. Then come back. I want to talk to you, young lady."

Biddy's smile faded. "All right," she said, and went to wash. She wondered why Aunt Hannah was not happy about the money.

"Bridget, explain to me where you got that money."

"Jock and I sold plums."

"But why? What did you want to buy?"

"I'm going to send it to China to help build a hospital," Biddy answered in a small, frightened voice.

"Biddy, you have disgraced me in the town. Good people don't go door to door selling things."

"I only wanted to help with the hospital," Biddy said, and began to cry.

"You are foolish to worry about the hospital. Your money will not do any good at all. After lunch you will go to your room and stay there the rest of the day. You must be punished for such actions."

Biddy was very quiet at lunch. After she had eaten, she said quietly, "Aunt Hannah, I didn't know it was naughty. I won't do it again."

"I forgive you, Biddy. From now on, you must try to be more careful in your actions."

Biddy sighed and went to her room. Sometimes she just didn't know what she ought to do. The thing that seemed right to her didn't seem right to Aunt Hannah.

Later on, Aunt Hannah called Maria. "Maria, when you take Biddy's tea tray up to her, take these picture books. I must make her stay in her room, but she felt so badly. This will help her pass the time."

"That's good of you, ma'am. She's so excited about the hospital project of her parents."

Aunt Hannah thought for a moment. "Yes, she is. Here. Take this box up to her. She can keep her money in it until she forgets about the silly hospital thing."

Maria took the box to Biddy when she took the tea tray.

"Oh, thank you Maria. This will be a big help to me."

Biddy did not know that Maria had quietly put in a gift toward the building of the hospital.

CHAPTER 8

LOST!

Jock was upset. Mrs. Brown said he must have gotten out on the wrong side of the bed, and that made him feel even more upset. He pushed the baby when she bumped into him. He didn't like his breakfast and wouldn't eat. Mrs. Brown told him to go outside and not come back in until he could be good.

Jock went out to find Biddy and met her coming down the road. They climbed a fence and wandered out through the fields. When they came to a fence post, Biddy took Froggy out of her coat pocket and set him up on top of it. "There, Froggy," she said. "Now you can see almost to China."

"You're silly to talk to that frog. He can't hear you."

"I know. But it's fun to pretend. Besides, he looks pretty sitting up in the sun. The light makes his eyes shine."

"Well, I think he looks silly. I'd like to throw him in the duck pond and see if the ducks would think he's so pretty. I think I will," he said, and grabbed the frog.

"No!" cried Biddy, but she was too late. Jock was off and running with the frog, and Biddy was running after him.

"Give me back my frog!" she screamed at him.

"You can't have him," Jock laughed, and kept on running as fast as he could.

Biddy began to catch up with Jock. She grabbed his coat and jerked him to a stop and began to pound him with her fists. "Give me Froggy! *Give me that frog*!" she demanded.

Suddenly Jock pulled free and quickly threw the frog into a tangle of blackberry bushes.

Biddy's eyes grew wide and frightened. She ran to the blackberry patch and looked in between the bushes, but she couldn't see the frog anywhere. She sat down on the ground and began to cry.

Jock was not cross any more. Now he felt sorry for what he had done. Quietly he walked to Biddy's side. "Don't cry, Biddy. I'll find him for you. I'm sorry."

Biddy stood up and wiped her eyes on her sleeve. She started into the bushes, but she had to go slowly because they pulled at her clothes and scratched her arms and legs. Jock plunged in after her, and together they looked for Froggy.

They looked and looked all morning, up and down the berry patch and all along the edges, but they could not find the lost frog. "Maybe I could buy a new one," Jock said hopefully.

"No," said Biddy. "It wouldn't be the same. That was the frog that Amah gave me, that her father gave her. Another one just wouldn't be the same."

Jock had to leave, and Biddy went off toward her house. She didn't walk very fast. She was too sad, thinking about her lost frog.

Maria met Biddy at the door. "My patience, Biddy, what have you been doing! Why, your legs and arms are all scratched and your dress is torn. Lucky for you your aunt is out, or you'd get a scolding."

Biddy began to cry. "Why, Biddy! What's the matter?" Maria stooped down and put her arm around Biddy's shoulder, but Biddy could not stop crying. After a little while, she was able to tell Maria what had happened.

"I guess I shouldn't have hit Jock," she sniffed. "Maybe he wouldn't have thrown the frog away."

"Now, Biddy, don't blame yourself. Jock was a bad boy to do that. I'll go out and try to find the frog after a while. Right now you must have some lunch and get some clean clothes on and take a short nap."

When Biddy was all alone in her room, she got quietly down on her knees and whispered, "Oh, please, Father in Heaven, forgive me for not fighting Giant Temper. I'm sorry I hit Jock. And please—please let me find Froggy. It would be so bad to lose him. Amen."

When Biddy's nap was over, Maria said that they would go together to look for the frog again. When they got there, they found Jock down on his hands and knees.

"Jock! You bad boy, what are you doing here?" scolded Maria.

"Don't scold, please," said Biddy. "Jock is sorry, aren't you?"

Jock hung his head and said that he was very sorry, and that he had come to look for the frog again. So all three began to look carefully all around the brier patch, but they could not find the frog.

"It's nearly half past four," said Maria, holding her back as she straightened up. "We'd better be going home. Your Aunt Hannah will be home at five. We'll have to come back tomorrow."

When Aunt Hannah returned, Maria met her at the door and motioned her into the kitchen to tell her about the lost frog. "I don't think Biddy could tell you," said Maria. "She's so sad that she starts to cry whenever she tries."

"Well, I think that Jock is a naughty boy. Maybe Bridget shouldn't play with him anymore."

"Oh, Biddy has forgiven him. And he may be able to help find the frog."

Aunt Hannah asked where the frog had been lost, and Maria tried to explain where they had looked. That evening Aunt Hannah herself went out into the woods to look for the frog, but she couldn't find it either. It seemed that the little green frog was gone forever.

CHAPTER 9

THE CATERPILLAR CATCHERS

When Biddy woke up the next morning, she suddenly thought, *Froggy is lost, and I might never see him again.* She was sad, but then she had another thought. *I never told Jock that I was sorry I hit him. I'll tell him that the first time I see him.*

When Jock came to play, Biddy told him that she was sorry. "I didn't fight Giant Temper. I forgot."

"That's all right," Jock said. "I'm sorry I threw away your frog."

"That's all right too. I didn't think I'd ever get over being mad at you for that, but Jesus helped me."

"You're funny. Do you think Jesus is real?"

"He's real," Biddy said. "He's my friend. I belong to Him."

"I guess I don't know much," Jock said with a sigh. "I wish I belonged to someone special. I'm going away to boarding school when summer's over, and I might be kind of lonesome."

"I got lonesome when I came to England, but then I remembered that Jesus is with me and I wasn't lonesome anymore. Jesus would be your friend if you want Him to be," said Biddy.

"Would He really?" asked Jock. Then he picked up a handful of stones and began throwing them away, one at a time. "Aw, I guess He wouldn't like me. You told me Jesus was always good, and I've been bad. He wouldn't want me."

"Yes He would, Jock!" Biddy exclaimed. "Listen. Let me tell you another Bible story. You know about Christmas?" Jock nodded his head. "Well, Jesus was born, and He grew up. He was really the Son of God, so He never did a bad thing. But when He was grownup, the people put Him up on a cross and He died."

"Why did they do that?" Jock asked.

"They didn't like Him because He was so good. It always reminded them that they

67

were bad. But when Jesus died, He really died for *us.*"

"Oh, I don't understand," said Jock, and began to throw the stones again.

"Just listen," Biddy said, and went on. "You said you were bad. I am too, lots of times. We're so bad that we really should die for our sin, those bad things we do. But Jesus knew about us even back then, and He died for us. He died so we wouldn't have to. God planned it that way so that if we would trust Jesus and believe that He really did that, we could be friends with Him and go to Heaven when we die."

"Where did you learn all that?" asked Jock.

"From my mommy and daddy. That's what they tell the Chinese people. And it's all true. It's in the Bible. I'll tell you a verse from the Bible. 'For God so loved the world, that he gave his only begotten Son, that whosoever believeth in him should not perish, but have everlasting life.'"

"And all I have to do is believe that Jesus really died for me, and He'll be my friend?"

Biddy nodded her head. "Besides that," she added, "He came to life again, and He'll never die. So when we belong to Him we'll come back to life after we die, and live forever in Heaven."

Jock's eyes were wide with surprise. "Really? I sure would like to have Him for my friend."

"Then you just pray and tell Him that you believe He died to take care of your sins, and you want to belong to Him forever."

And so Jock bowed his head, as he had seen Biddy do, and talked to Jesus. "Jesus, I just found out what You did. Thank You. I guess You wouldn't want a bad boy to be Your friend, so I'm glad You took care of all that when You died. I want to belong to You, and if You can, help me to be good. I'd like to be Your friend."

Jock raised his head and looked around. "Did He hear me?" he asked Biddy.

"Oh, yes! He's right here with us, even if you can't see Him. Jock, now you're God's child, just like I am."

Jock grinned. "This is going to be fun, having a friend who never goes away. Let's go tell someone!"

So off they went to visit Mr. and Mrs. Camp. They met Mr. Camp coming down the road with his shovel in his hand.

"Hello, Mr. Camp. How is your bad leg?" asked Biddy.

"It's better, thanks." Then he noticed Jock's big grin. "What are you so happy about, young man?" he asked.

"I've got a new friend. I belong to Jesus now, just like Biddy does."

"Well, that's fine," said Mr. Camp. He didn't know what else to say, so he asked Biddy if her parents had written to her from China.

"Not yet. It takes a long time to get a letter. Mr. Camp, where do people get money in England?"

"You have to get a job and work for it. Do you want some money?"

"Yes, I want to save some to send to Mommy and Daddy for the hospital in China."

"Why don't you go to Mr. Brown's farm and see if he has some job that two young folks could handle?"

"Come on, Biddy," Jock said, pulling at Biddy's sleeve. "I know where Mr. Brown is. We'll go and ask him. Thank you, Mr. Camp!" They ran off down the road, waving to him.

They found Mr. Brown in the barn feeding his cattle. "Well," he said, rubbing his chin. "So you want to earn some money for a hospital, do you? Can you catch caterpillars?"

Biddy wrinkled up her nose, but Jock said, "Yes, we can!"

Mr. Brown told them that the cabbage patch was being eaten up by caterpillars, and that he would pay them one penny for each caterpillar they caught. Jock got a box to put them in, and off they went to the cabbage patch.

Jock began pulling off the fuzzy little worms and dropping them into the box. "Hurry, Biddy," he urged. "The more we get, the more money you can send for the hospital."

Biddy didn't like the caterpillars, so she carefully picked them off with two fingers and quickly dropped them into the box. She didn't get as many as Jock, but she kept at it, even though she was a little afraid of the fuzzy things.

"Say, you did a good job!" said Jock. "You aren't such a fraidycat after all." That made Biddy feel better, and she got one more caterpillar just before they headed back toward the farm buildings to show Mr. Brown their box.

They had caught one hundred and thirty-two caterpillars, so Mr. Brown paid them one dollar and thirty-two cents.

"That won't build any hospital," he said, "but it's a start."

Biddy took the money, since Jock was glad to let her have all of it. She took it home and put it in the box that Aunt Hannah had given her, and then she went out to play with Jock again.

"I've been thinking about your frog," said Jock. "Do you think you'll ever find him?"

"I will. Jesus will help me. I don't know how or when I'll get him back, but I'm sure that Jesus will send him."

CHAPTER 10

MONEY FOR THE HOSPITAL

Jock was at the door knocking before Biddy had finished her breakfast. Maria answered the door.

"Why, Jock, what an early bird you are!"

"Good morning, Maria. May I speak to Biddy, please?"

"She's not finished with her breakfast yet. Have you had yours?"

"Yes ma'am, but I think I could still eat some more."

Maria laughed. "Come in the kitchen and you can have some hot chocolate and toast and jelly." Maria poured hot chocolate for Jock as he climbed up on the high kitchen stool. "Why are you so early?" she asked.

"Biddy wants to earn money for her parents to build a hospital with. Yesterday we caught caterpillars and made one dollar and thirty-two cents. I came over to tell her that we can work for Mrs. Brown today."

"How nice! Are you looking for some more jobs?"

"Yes we are. Do you have something for us?"

"Well, I'll be doing some baking today, and I'll need some help with the extra dishes."

"Ugh!" Jock scowled. "I don't much like doing dishes, but if Biddy can catch caterpillars, I guess I can do it."

"Do what?" asked Biddy as she came into the kitchen.

"Wash dishes," said Jock. "Come on. I'll tell you all the plans." He pulled her toward the door. "We'll be back later, Maria. Save the dishes for us!"

Once outside, Jock shared his good news. "We can make lots of money, Biddy! There are all kinds of jobs we can do." They hurried off to the farm to see what Mrs. Brown had for them to do.

"I have to go into town today and do some shopping. I'd like to have you children play with the baby and keep her happy until I come back."

"That will be fun," said Biddy.

"Well, we'll see about that," said Mrs. Brown as she picked up her purse. "I'll be back in about three hours."

As soon as Mrs. Brown closed the door, baby Amy began to cry. "Oh, don't cry, Amy. Here! Play with this ball." Jock handed her a bright red ball, but Amy just slapped at it and cried harder.

"Maybe we could find something for her to eat," said Biddy. "A cracker or a cookie." They found some soft cookies in the cookie jar and gave one to Amy. Soon she stopped crying and began to play with her toys.

While she played, Jock and Biddy talked about things that they could do to make more money.

"This is lots more fun than making money for yourself," Jock said. "Especially when I know that it will help to let other people learn about Jesus."

Biddy thought of all the people who would come to the hospital to get well and who would hear about the Lord Jesus. "We might have to work a long time. I think it takes a lot of money to build a hospital."

Soon Mrs. Brown was home. She laughed when she saw the cookie crumbs on Amy's face.

"It looks like Biddy and Jock know how to make a baby happy," she said.

"If there's anything else we can do for you, we'd be glad to help," offered Biddy.

"Do you know how to sew?" asked Mrs. Brown.

"I can sew a little," said Biddy. "Buttons and hems and seams."

"You wait right here," said Mrs. Brown. "I'll be right back."

When she returned, she was carrying a small yellow basket with shirts in it. "If you'll sew on the missing buttons and fix the tears in the pockets, I'd be glad to pay you for your help," she said.

"Oh, thank you!" exclaimed Biddy. "I'll be very careful and try to do a good job."

Mrs. Brown gave them each a dollar and they ran off to help Maria wash dishes.

"I've never seen two children work so hard," said Maria. Jock stood on a chair at the sink with a big apron tied around his waist. He was scrubbing a sticky pan. Biddy was drying plates and glass baking dishes. "We want to get lots of money for the hospital," she said.

Just then Aunt Hannah came into the kitchen. "Biddy! Jock! What are you doing?"

Biddy looked frightened. She had forgotten that Aunt Hannah had been angry when they sold plums in town.

Maria answered Aunt Hannah. "They've come to help me, ma'am," said Maria. "I'll pay them from my own money. It's for the hospital."

"Oh, yes. I'd forgotten about that. Well, I suppose this is a much better way than having you go all around town selling plums. And you really are helping. Just don't let your ambitions turn into greed."

"We won't," said Biddy. "It's God's money, so that people can hear about Jesus."

When the dishes were done and the kitchen was all clean, Maria gave them blueberry pie and one whole dollar each!

CHAPTER 11

HELPING MRS. CAMP

After the children had finished helping Maria, they still had time to visit the Camps before supper. Jock and Biddy ran down the road to the little white house and knocked at the kitchen door.

"Good afternoon, Mrs. Camp." Jock said in his most polite voice when she came to the door. "We came to see if there are any jobs we could do for you."

"We're earning money for a hospital in China," Biddy added.

"Well, what a surprise! Come into the kitchen. You can help me right now." When the children came inside, they saw—a large pile of dirty dishes at the sink!

"Is *that* the job you have for us?" Jock asked.

Mrs. Camp nodded. Jock didn't look very happy, but he and Biddy began working. The pile of dirty dishes grew smaller and smaller and the pile of clean dishes grew larger and larger.

"That's a fine job," said Mrs. Camp. "Would you children like to stay and have supper with Mr. Camp and me?"

"Oh, could we?" Biddy asked excitedly. "I've never eaten away from Aunt Hannah's house since I came to England. Please call and ask if I may stay."

"And please call Mrs. Brown too," said Jock.

They waited impatiently while Mrs. Camp made her calls. Then she came back with the news. "You may both stay," she said.

While they ate, Jock told Mrs. Camp about catching caterpillars, but she said she didn't like to hear about caterpillars while she was having supper.

Biddy told Mr. Camp about the sewing that she was doing for Mrs. Brown, but he didn't seem to care about sewing at all.

Biddy looked out the window just as the sun touched the hill behind God's garden. "I think we'd better hurry, Jock," she said. "May we be excused?" she asked.

"Yes, of course," said Mrs. Camp. "Go right home now, or your people won't let you come to visit anymore. Would you like to come back and help me work in the garden tomorrow? Things are getting ripe so fast that I can't keep up."

"We'd love to, Mrs. Camp!" they said together. Then they hurried outside and up the road.

"Say!" said Jock. "Mrs. Camp didn't give us any money for doing all those dishes."

"No, but she gave us a fine supper—with gingerbread for dessert."

"You can't send gingerbread to China and build a hospital with it," Jock said.

"I know. But I think Jesus is pleased if we help people, even if we don't get paid. Pleasing Jesus is what's important."

"You're right," said Jock. "I've been trying to please Him since we're friends now."

"I'm glad you're helping me earn money for the hospital," said Biddy as she went into her own yard.

"It's fun," said Jock. He waved goodbye as he ran up the road. "I'll see you tomorrow!"

They were at Mrs. Camp's garden bright and early the next morning.

"First we have to pick all the ripe vegetables," said Mrs. Camp. Biddy didn't know very much about vegetables, so she carried the basket while Jock picked. First they picked tomatoes, then peppers, corn, and squash. Then they pulled carrots, turnips, and potatoes out of the ground. Then they picked beans and peas. Biddy and Jock were so tired that they could hardly walk to the house when Mrs. Camp announced it was time to eat some lunch.

After big glasses of milk plus sandwiches and cookies, Jock and Biddy felt much better. They were proud to see the piles of fresh vegetables. Mrs. Camp would sell some of them, put some of them in jars, and keep some to use fresh. She was glad to have them all picked, and Biddy and Jock were glad they had helped.

"Would you like to tell us one of your stories, Biddy?" asked Mrs. Camp.

"Tell us one about China," said Jock. "Tell us the one about the green frog again."

So Biddy told the story of how the green frog came to Amah. "Oh!" said Mrs. Camp. "I almost forgot to pay you for your work. Hearing about China made me think about the hospital, and that made me think about the money." She got up from the table and went to her kitchen cupboard and took down a little metal box. She pulled out four one-dollar bills. She gave two to Jock and two to Biddy.

"Thank you very much!" they said. They were surprised to be paid so much.

"You worked hard for it," said Mrs. Camp. "And I'm glad you are trying to help those poor people in China."

"We want them to know about Jesus," said Biddy. "Isn't that what you want too?"

"Yes," said Mrs. Camp. "You know, Biddy, since you and Jock came to visit me, I've been thinking about the Lord Jesus a lot more often. I didn't always try to please Him the way you do. But now I want to do just that. Now I think you had better go and play. You've worked enough for one day."

So off they went with a handful of cookies each. Biddy said goodbye to Jock and went in through the kitchen. And there, on the table, sat the little green frog!

CHAPTER 12

THE WALLET

"My frog!" Biddy shouted. She ran to the table, picked up the frog, and put it up to her face. "Where did you come from?"

Maria had been watching. "Where would you guess that it came from?" asked Maria.

"Jesus sent him back somehow," Biddy answered. "I asked Him to do it, and He did."

"Well, you might be right at that." Then Maria told Biddy how a poor beggar woman had come to the door selling things that she had found. Maria had seen the frog in the basket and bought it from the woman.

"That was Jesus sending Froggy back. He doesn't always do things just like we think He will, but He always gets things done. Don't you believe that Jesus did it, Maria?"

Maria thought for a moment. "Yes," she said slowly, "I think I *do* believe that this little frog really came from Him. Remember how hard we all looked, and we didn't find him? Now here he is. I guess Jesus must have sent him, just as you say."

Biddy was so happy to have the frog back that she took him right up to her room and put him on a shelf where she could see him all the time. "I guess I won't take him outside anymore. I don't want to lose him again," she said. She went to the Brown's farm to tell Jock the good news, then came home for supper.

A couple of days later, Biddy didn't feel well when she got up. She had a headache and she felt cold and very tired. She didn't want to eat any breakfast. Aunt Hannah was in such a hurry to go out and take care of some business that she didn't notice that Biddy didn't seem to be well. Aunt Hannah had already eaten her breakfast, so she said goodbye to Biddy and was on her way.

Biddy went outside where Jock was waiting to play, but she didn't feel like playing. When Jock threw the ball to her, she couldn't catch it. Her arms seemed too tired to hold it. She was too tired to run. Her knees felt weak and shaky.

"You're sick, Biddy. You ought to go home and go to bed."

"I think I just have a cold, Jock," Biddy said. "But maybe I will go home. I don't feel like playing. It isn't much fun being outside."

So Jock went back to the farm, and Biddy went to her house. She walked slowly, because her legs were so shaky. She looked down at her feet while she walked. Suddenly she saw something lying in the road right in front of her feet. It was made of leather, she discovered. It was a wallet. When she opened it, the first thing she noticed was that there was a lot of money in it. Not just one-dollar bills, like she and Jock had earned, but ten-dollar bills, twenty-dollar bills, and even a fifty-dollar bill!

There were a lot of cards and papers in the wallet too, but Biddy did not wait to look at those. She kept walking to her house because she began feeling worse. She carried the wallet in both hands because she didn't want to lose it. Her thoughts were mixed up. She thought of what Amah had told her; that there was a lot of money in England. Maybe this was what Amah had meant. But this was someone else's money. He had earned it, just as Biddy and Jock had earned theirs. But she was too tired and sick to think about it. When she got to the house, she went right to her room. She put the wallet in a dresser drawer, underneath one of her silk dresses that she had brought from China. Then she lay down on her bed.

Soon Maria came to the door. "Biddy! I didn't even hear you come in. I just came to bring some clean sheets. What's the matter?"

"I don't know," she said. Her throat was scratchy and dry. "I don't feel good."

Maria came and placed her hand on Biddy's forehead. "You have a fever. You'd better get into bed and I'll bring you some hot soup for lunch."

"I don't want anything. My head aches. And I don't want to stand up."

Maria helped Biddy get her pajamas on and get into bed, then went downstairs to call Aunt Hannah. She had just reached the phone when she heard a knock at the door. It was Jock.

"Hello, Maria—"

"I'm sorry, Jock," Maria interrupted, "but Biddy can't come out. She's sick."

"I know. I came to tell you that Amy's got the measles. Maybe that's what's wrong with Biddy. We took care of Amy the other day."

"The measles! I suppose that's what it is. Thank you for telling me, Jock. Will you get them too?"

"I had them already when I was only little," he said.

He said goodbye and Maria called Aunt Hannah. She came home as soon as she could and went upstairs to see Biddy. There was Biddy, her face and arms covered with tiny red spots.

Biddy didn't want to talk at all, because her throat was sore, and she was so sleepy. She slept and slept, dreaming about China and her mother. Sometimes she thought that Maria was Amah. The doctor came. Biddy was half-asleep, half-awake, and she heard the doctor say that she was having a very hard case of the measles, and that she would be sick for at least a week! But Biddy didn't even care. All she wanted to do was stay in bed.

Each morning Aunt Hannah had breakfast alone. She missed Biddy, and sometimes she wished she had been a little nicer to Biddy. She knew Biddy tried to be good. It was just that sometimes she didn't know the right thing to do. One morning when the house seemed especially quiet, Aunt Hannah called Maria to share the news in the morning paper.

"Look at this, Maria. Mr. Digby has lost his wallet."

"Mr. Digby? That rich old man from the Grange?"

"Yes. He offered a large reward. I'm sure it will be found soon. Everyone will want the money."

Aunt Hannah was right. Everyone in the town looked in their yards. They went out on the road looking. Some said they thought

91

they had seen it, but couldn't remember where. Others were sure it had been stolen. Even the police couldn't find it, or find anyone who had it. But Biddy didn't know about the lost wallet or the reward. She never even thought about the folded leather wallet hidden in her dresser drawer.

After another week she began to feel better and asked if she could go out and play. "Not yet," said Aunt Hannah. "You are still sick, even though you feel much better. But you can come downstairs and eat lunch if you want to."

Biddy was eager to get out of bed, but when she did, she found that her legs had forgotten how to stand up. She sat down on the floor, feeling dizzy. Then she laughed. She felt silly sitting there in a heap. Aunt Hannah laughed too and helped her get up. "Why, Biddy," she said with a chuckle, "have you forgotten how to walk?"

Aunt Hannah took a clean dress from Biddy's closet for her to put on, then went to the dresser to get a fresh hair ribbon. There she noticed the lovely silk dress that had come from China. "I hope this will be all right in the drawer," she said. "If it gets dirty or creased, it will be ruined." She lifted it out, and there, underneath the dress, lay the wallet.

"Biddy, what is this?" she asked as she took it out.

"Oh, I found that."

"And you didn't tell anyone? You were going to keep it for yourself?"

"No, the hospital—"

"The hospital? You were going to send stolen money to China to build a hospital? Didn't your parents teach you that it is wrong to steal? I'm ashamed of you, Biddy!" Aunt Hannah was very upset. She didn't know what to say or do.

"But I just found it—"

"That doesn't mean it's yours. All those people in town. If they find out this wallet was in my house, I'll never be able to face them. What will I do." She closed her eyes and thought for a moment. Then she said quickly, "Get dressed, Biddy. You are going to see Mr. Digby. This wallet belongs to him, and you will have to tell him what you have done."

"I didn't mean to be naughty, Aunt Hannah." Biddy was beginning to cry.

"Don't try to make excuses," Aunt Hannah said sharply. "You hid the wallet and didn't tell anyone because you wanted to send the money to China for that silly hospital. I thought you were trying to be good, but evidently I was wrong."

Aunt Hannah went downstairs to call a taxi while Biddy finished dressing. When she was ready to go, she got her frog down from the shelf. *If only Amah were here,* she thought. But Amah was a long ways away. Then she remembered that Jesus was always beside her, so she talked to Him. "Dear Jesus, I didn't know it was wrong. I didn't mean to steal. Please help me be brave. And don't let Mr. Digby send me to prison, or I won't be able to make any more money for the hospital."

"Bridget, the taxi is here," called Aunt Hannah. "Come down at once."

Biddy's legs were still shaky, but she didn't know if it was because she was sick or because she was afraid. Aunt Hannah sat very straight in the back seat of the taxi, holding the wallet tightly. Biddy held the frog in her lap and wished that she had never come to England!

CHAPTER 13

AN IMPORTANT DISCOVERY

The taxi pulled up in front of a big house. It was much bigger than Aunt Hannah's house, and there were three big barns behind the house, with lots of neat white fences. There was a long gravel walk lined with flowers that led to the big front door. Biddy whispered a prayer again as they got out of the taxi. "Please, Jesus, help Mr. Digby to understand." Aunt Hannah told the taxi driver to wait. Then they began the long walk up to the house. Biddy wanted to hold Aunt Hannah's hand, but Aunt Hannah was holding the wallet and would not put her hand down where Biddy could reach it.

At last they came to the big door. Aunt Hannah rang the bell. They could hear chimes sounding inside. Then a man in a black suit opened the door. "Good morning, madam," he said, "May I help you?"

"Is Mr. Digby in? We have a matter of business to discuss with him."

The man said that Mr. Digby was in, and asked them to come inside. They walked down a long hall, past many doors, and finally stopped. The man opened the door and announced, "The Misses Forrester to see you, sir."

Mr. Digby was seated in a large, soft chair beside a fireplace, reading a book. He stood up and came to meet them. "How are you, Miss Forrester," he said to Aunt Hannah. She answered that she was fine, but that she had some business and really didn't have much time. Then Mr. Digby saw Biddy and recognized her. "Well, well! My little friend from China. And how are *you*?"

"I had the measles."

"That is a shame, isn't it. You know, I've been waiting for you to come and visit me. I've been away for some time now, but I didn't forget that invitation, and I really meant for you to come sooner. I'm glad that you're finally here."

"I didn't know that you and Bridget were acquainted, Mr. Digby," said Aunt Hannah with a surprised look on her face.

Mr. Digby smiled. "Oh, yes. We are quite good friends, aren't we, Biddy?"

Biddy nodded her head, but her lip was trembling, and tears were beginning to come to her eyes.

"Mr. Digby," Aunt Hannah began impatiently, "Biddy has done something very wrong." She handed the wallet to him. "Biddy has had this in her dresser drawer for some time. She did not tell anyone about it. I feel disgraced that one of my own family would do this, and that it has been in my house all this time, causing you worry and inconvenience."

"Well, this is strange. You don't look like a thief, little miss. Perhaps we should have a talk about this. Miss Forrester, if you would like to leave us alone, my chauffeur will drive Biddy home later."

"If that is what you want. I certainly hope you can show Bridget that in England there are laws. I seem to have failed." She left the room. By now, Biddy was crying quite hard.

Mr. Digby brought up a smaller chair for her to sit on near him and near the fire. He took her hand and led her to the chair, while she tried to stop the tears. Finally she stopped and he said, "Now, tell me all about what happened."

"I—I was sick. I had the measles, but I didn't know right then. I went out to play with Jock, and I found your wallet in the road with lots of money in it. First I thought God sent it to me, 'cause I've been trying to make money to send to the hospital in China. But I knew it belonged to somebody else first, and I didn't know what to do. And then I got real sick and forgot about it. Aunt Hannah found it today and thought I took it on purpose. She wouldn't listen to me."

"I see. Aunt Hannah didn't want you to get into any trouble over it, and that is good. And it is good that you came to see me. You mentioned a hospital in China. Where is it, and who manages such a place?"

"It isn't built yet. My mommy and daddy work in China, but they only have a clinic, no hospital. Amah told me that when I came to England, I'd find lots of money, and that I could send it to China to build a hospital. Jock has been helping me. We have quite a bit already. We sold plums and caught caterpillars and babysat—that's how I got the measles."

Mr. Digby laughed. "You have been busy! So you wanted to send the money to China for a hospital. Tell me, did your Aunt Hannah tell you about the reward that was offered for the return of the wallet?"

"No," answered Biddy.

"How much money have you and Jock made for the hospital?" he asked.

Biddy thought. "There was the plums, two dollars and seventy-three cents. And there was caterpillars, a dollar and thirty-two cents, and baby-sitting, a dollar each, and sewing, one dollar, and Maria and Mrs. Camp, that was six dollars. How much is that all together?"

"That's over thirteen dollars," said Mr. Digby. "You've worked hard, haven't you?" Biddy nodded. "Well, the reward is almost five times that much. The reward is sixty dollars. What will you do with that? It is your's because you returned the wallet, after taking good care of it all this time."

"Oh, I'll send it to China," said Biddy happily. "That should be enough to build a hospital, don't you think?"

"Not quite," said Mr. Digby, laughing. "Don't you want to buy anything for yourself?"

"I have lots of things. The Chinese people don't have anything at all. They get sick all the time. I'd rather give the money to build a hospital. Besides, then they can hear about Jesus."

"Do you know about Jesus?" asked Mr. Digby.

"Oh, yes. He's my very best friend. I asked Him to help you to understand, and He did, didn't He? And Jock believes in Jesus too. Just the other day he asked Jesus to be His friend."

"Do you know that you should have told someone about the wallet?"

Biddy's head drooped a little. "Yes. I should have told Maria right away. I guess I wanted the money too much."

"It is wrong to get things in the wrong way, even if it is for a good cause. But I know you did not mean to keep the wallet for yourself, and so I am going to give the reward money to you. Do you want to take it with you when you go?"

"If I may, please. I have a box that I'm keeping the money in. Sixty dollars will fill it up."

"That's enough business," said Mr. Digby, leaning back. "Tell me all about China."

Biddy told him about her parents' clinic, about Amah, and about her frog.

"I've been noticing that frog," said Mr. Digby. "He looks like he might be worth a lot of money. You should be careful not to lose him."

"I did lose him once. Jock was mad— before he had Jesus to help him fight Giant Temper—and he threw Froggy into the woods. But God brought him back to me. Amah gave him to me, and I wouldn't want to lose him."

"Would you loan Froggy to me for a few days? I have a friend who knows about Chinese jade, and he would know if Froggy is made out of jade or some other stone. It might be that you could sell Froggy and get quite a lot of money for your hospital."

Biddy looked down at the frog. "I don't know if I could do that," she said quietly.

"Would you like me to find out if he is valuable? Then you can decide what to do with him."

Biddy nodded and handed the frog to Mr. Digby, who placed it on the mantlepiece over the fireplace. When he stood up, Biddy noticed that the book he had been reading when they came in was a Bible.

"Mr. Digby," she exclaimed. "You're reading the Bible. Is Jesus your friend too?"

"He certainly is," said Mr. Digby with a smile. "We have been friends for a long time."

"I'm glad. I'm glad I came to see you, even if I was afraid."

"Well, you're not afraid anymore. Why don't we go and see what Mrs. Prentiss is having for lunch today? She is my housekeeper, and she's a fine cook."

Together they walked down the long hall and into a small dining room, where a friendly lady in a red and white dress brought them their lunch. After they had eaten, Mr. Digby took Biddy all around the large farm. She rode a horse, and played with the dogs, and looked at Mr. Digby's collection of rare birds.

"Jock would like to see all of your animals. He lives on the Browns' farm and likes it very much."

"The next time you come to visit me, you may bring him along. I'm sure he's a fine boy."

"I think I'd better go now," said Biddy. "Aunt Hannah wouldn't want me to stay too long."

"All right. Come inside and I'll give you your reward money. I'll write a note to your aunt so that she will know that I understand what happened and that the money is to be yours."

"Thank you very much," she said. "I try to be good, but Aunt Hannah doesn't always understand."

"Your Aunt Hannah hasn't had a little girl in her house before. I have. I know what little girls like. My little girl went to be with her mother and the Lord Jesus in Heaven, but I remember quite well what it is like to have children in the house. You must try to help your Aunt Hannah. She is learning something new."—

"I'll try harder, Mr. Digby. She's very nice to me."

"Perhaps your Aunt Hannah needs to learn about the Lord Jesus too. We shall have to pray for her, won't we?"

Biddy nodded, and they went into the house again. Soon Biddy was on her way home in a big car, with a check for sixty dollars in one hand and a note from Mr. Digby in the other hand. Biddy wondered what Aunt Hannah would think.

Aunt Hannah was at her desk. Biddy came in slowly and stood away from her. When she turned around, Biddy handed her the note from Mr. Digby and also the check.

Aunt Hannah read the note carefully, a frown on her face. Finally she sighed deeply. "Mr. Digby said that you were a delightful guest and a fine girl, that you never intended to keep the money for yourself, and that the reward money is yours. I'm afraid I must say that I am sorry, Biddy. I was very unkind to you."

"That's all right, Aunt Hannah. You were trying to do what was right."

"Thank you for your forgiveness, Biddy. I think we should open an account at the bank for you. This check will be a good start toward your education in the future."

"Oh, no!" Biddy said quickly. "I want it for the hospital in China. Mr. Digby said I could use it for that."

"Well, we shall have to write and ask your parents about that. Meanwhile, we'll put all your money in the bank, where it will be safe. Don't you think that is a good idea?"

"I don't know. I just want it to get to China."

"Don't worry about that now." Aunt Hannah looked at Biddy's pockets and at her hands. "Where is your frog? Have you lost him again?"

"No, Mr. Digby asked to borrow him for a day or two. He wants to find out if Froggy is worth money."

Aunt Hannah was surprised. "If I had had any idea he was valuable, I would have been more careful of where you took him," she said.

Biddy had to go to bed early that night, because she still wasn't all over the measles. What an exciting day it had been. She wondered about her frog. What would she do if he was worth a lot of money? And she was so glad to find out that Mr. Digby loved Jesus, and that he had been kind to her. And Jock was invited to come and see the farm! With so many good thoughts in her mind, Biddy fell asleep quickly.

CHAPTER 14

EVERYONE'S HOSPITAL

From then on it seemed that everyone was interested in the hospital. Biddy prayed every day that Jesus would help her not to be selfish with her money, but to remember that it was all for the hospital so the Chinese could hear about Jesus. She tried to sew neatly when Aunt Hannah taught her new stitches. Then she could offer to sew for other people in the neighborhood. Even though she would rather be outside playing, she would sit inside and sew. She often cared for little Amy. That way she was a help to Mrs. Brown, and was also able to make a little more money for the hospital.

The little box in her room got heavier and heavier. Biddy didn't count the money. She wanted to surprise herself when the time came to send it to China. Aunt Hannah had put most of the money in the bank, and Biddy kept only the coins that she earned.

One day Jock came to the door. When Biddy opened the door, he quickly handed her a handful of coins.

"Where did you get it?" asked Biddy with a surprised look.

Jock was grinning widely. "I worked for it. You're not the only one who cares about the hospital."

They went outside into the garden to play catch. "But what did you do? You don't have a job, do you?"

"Mr. Brown decided to pay me for helping him. He said I was such good help that it was worth the price, and if I was his own son, he would still pay me. I've been helping with all the chores, and learned an awful lot about the farm."

Jock told her about feeding the animals and milking the cows, about cutting hay and harvesting wheat. "I wish I lived on a farm," Biddy said. "I'd rather make money doing things outdoors than by sewing."

"You couldn't do farm work," said Jock. "That's for boys. Girls are supposed to sew.

Besides, if nobody sewed, I wouldn't have buttons on my shirt."

"I guess you're right. Would you like to come and see how much money I have for the hospital, besides what's in the bank?"

Together they went upstairs to shake the box and guess at how much was in it. Jock took the money out of his pocket, where he had put it when they went to play catch, and dropped it into the box, one coin at a time.

Maria heard them laughing. She stopped her cooking to go and see what they were doing.

"Hello, Maria," said Biddy when Maria came to the door. "This is all hospital money. Jock just brought some more."

"That's good. Soon it will be built, don't you think so?" Maria smiled and winked.

"I think it will, Maria. I really do."

Maria turned away and went back downstairs. She felt guilty. She had thought that soon Biddy would forget about the hospital and begin to spend the money for herself. Now Jock was saving his money too!

Maria thought back to the days when she was a child and used to go to church and Sunday school with her mother. She had heard about people across the sea who knew nothing about Jesus, who were poor and sick, but she didn't care about them as much as Biddy did. She couldn't go to those countries now, but she did have some money saved—

She went to her room and found her own small bank where she kept all her extra money. She counted it carefully, then looked at her bankbook to see how much money she had in the bank. Then she did something that she had not done in a long time. She got down on her knees and told the Lord Jesus that all her money was His, and that from then on, she would try to please Him in all she did.

Biddy and Jock had gone outside, so Maria quietly took the money into Biddy's room and put it in the box, then wrote a check for all the money that was in her bank account and put that in the box. She went back to her work feeling happier than she had in many years.

Biddy and Jock were walking up the road toward the farm a few days later when they met Mr. Digby coming down the road toward them. The children ran to meet him.

"Have you brought my frog back, Mr. Digby?" asked Biddy.

"Yes I have, little miss, and I have some very important news for you and your Aunt Hannah. Tell me, how is your hospital fund coming along? Have you been catching any more caterpillars?"

Biddy wrinkled up her nose and Jock laughed. "We haven't been catching caterpillars, but we've been doing lots of other things."

They told him all the work they had been doing, as they walked toward Biddy's house.

"My Aunt Hannah is out right now, Mr. Digby. Can you wait until she comes back? I'm so anxious to hear the news. Won't you tell me?"

"That's a secret until your aunt comes home. I'm sure you can wait that long.

Here." He handed her the green frog, which he had been carrying in his pocket. "Would you like to take care of this little friend? Put him where he won't get lost."

"I can guess! I can guess!" sang Biddy. Froggy is worth a lot of money, isn't he? Maybe even fifty dollars!"

"Now you've guessed," said Mr. Digby with a laugh. "But I won't tell you exactly how much he's worth until your aunt comes home."

Jock's eyes were wide with surprise. "Froggy is worth money? And I threw him away!" He sat shaking his head.

Just then Aunt Hannah came in the door.

"Why, Mr. Digby, what a surprise to see you here. What can I do for you?"

"It's something that I can do for you, Miss Forrester," he said as he stood. "or at least for Biddy and her parents. I have quite a story to tell you."

They all sat down while Maria brought in tea. "My friend is an expert in Oriental jade. He said that Biddy's frog is well over three hundred years old and comes from one of the temples in the hills of the Chinese inland country."

"That's where Amah lived," said Biddy.

"And the man who brought the frog took it from the temple, I suppose," continued Mr. Digby. "The eyes are real diamonds— small, but of a good quality. Of course, the frog would have to be taken to London to be sold, perhaps to the museum or to some private collector. But we haven't asked the owner, have we. What do you say, Biddy; do you want to sell the frog?"

"How much could your friend get for the frog?" asked Biddy.

"Eight hundred dollars, at the least," said Mr. Digby.

Jock and Biddy stared at each other, their mouths open. "How much is eight hundred dollars?" Biddy whispered.

"A lot," Jock whispered back. "I never saw that much."

Biddy only had to think for a minute. The frog had been a special gift from Amah. She wanted to keep it forever. But Amah would understand, and Biddy could always remember Amah even without the frog.

"I want to sell Froggy," she said, and then Jock gave out a cheer.

"Good for you, Biddy," Mr. Digby said. "I know the frog was important to you, but you love Jesus and the Chinese people more than the frog, don't you? Now I have some more news for you. I've been thinking about your hospital and about your parents. I have a lot of money that I haven't decided on a use for. Since you have worked so hard for the hospital, I will supply all the money that is needed above what you have saved."

Biddy was so happy and so excited that she couldn't even talk. She and Jock jumped around the room laughing and singing. Aunt Hannah watched them quietly.

"Mr. Digby, I don't really understand why you are doing all this, but it is your money."

"Miss Forrester, do you love the Lord Jesus? I do. I want others to hear about His love. Besides, I spent many years in China and never gave anything back to the country, though I earned a lot of money there. Don't you feel sympathetic to the work that your brother and sister-in-law are doing?"

"I really haven't thought much about it. I think that if they want to go and spend their lives in such an unbearable country, that is their business. I am teaching their child. That is enough help."

"It seems that you don't care if the Chinese people die or not. Tell me, do you know the Lord Jesus as your Saviour?"

"I am a good woman. I lead a good life," said Aunt Hannah coldly.

"You should learn from your little niece," said Mr. Digby as he stood. "She loves Him with all her heart, and you can see what a fine girl she is. I must be going. Think about the matter, Miss Forrester. My friend will be by for the frog in a few days. I suggest that you write a letter to Biddy's parents telling them of the plans, and find out how much they need for their hospital. Goodbye." Biddy and Jock waved from the window till Mr. Digby was out of sight.

"May we go to see the Camps?" asked Biddy.

"Yes, if you don't stay too long. Be back in time for supper," said Aunt Hannah.

Off they went to tell all the news to Mr. and Mrs. Camp. "And Froggy is worth eight hundred dollars!" said Biddy again.

"That's a lot of money. Biddy, I don't have much money, but I would like to give something." She got the box down from the cupboard. "Here is ten dollars. Please take it and send it along with the other money. The Lord will know that I gave it from a willing heart."

Mr. Camp had been quiet the whole time Biddy told her news. Now he spoke furiously. "I suppose you think I'm going to give you some money too, just so I can feel like I'm helping God a little. Well, I'm not. I haven't done anything for God all these years, and I'm not going to start. He hasn't done anything for me."

Biddy looked frightened. "I didn't want you to think we were asking for money, Mr. Camp. God doesn't want you to give Him your money unless you love Him." They were all quiet for a moment. Then Biddy spoke again. "Mr. Camp, God has done something for you. Do you know what?" He did not answer, so Biddy continued. "God sent His Son, Jesus, to die on the cross for you so that you could go to Heaven, even if you have been very naughty. God will forgive you if you ask Him to. Isn't that a lot to do for you?"

Still Mr. Camp was quiet. At last he sighed. "Yes, Biddy, I think you're right. I got angry with you because you were doing the right thing, and I was too proud to admit that I was wrong. I must do just what you said. I must ask Jesus to come and live in my life and make me good." Mrs. Camp squeezed his hand. "I guess I'll have to do some more thinking about that hospital in China." He smiled at Biddy and Jock.

Biddy and Jock had to go home, though they would have liked to stay with the Camps a little longer. "Just look, Jock," Biddy said as they walked along together. "Jesus saved an old man like Mr. Camp, and a boy like you, and He's made everyone interested in the hospital. Everything is just too good to be true."

When Biddy got home, she went to ask Aunt Hannah if she could have paper to write a letter to China. She found Aunt Hannah in her own room, looking at some very pretty jewelry.

"Aunt Hannah, I'd like to write to Mommy and Daddy before we have supper. May I have some paper?"

"Yes, you may get it from my desk, Biddy, in the middle drawer." Biddy turned to go, but Aunt Hannah called her. "I—I thought you might like to know," she said with a faint smile, "I've decided to sell this jewelry and give the money to the hospital. I've been a very proud woman and never gave a thought to the Lord and all that He had done for me. Thank you for helping me to find Him."

Biddy ran to her aunt and put her arms around her. "I'm so happy I could just *bust!*" she cried.

"*Burst,* Biddy, not bust," corrected Aunt Hannah, and then they both laughed and went downstairs together to eat.

The whole house seemed to be a nicer place now. So many things had happened since Biddy came to England! She sat down to write a long letter to her mommy and daddy.

CHAPTER 15

THE SECRET

Dear Mommy and Daddy,

I have some good news for you. You can build a hospital in China now, because we have lots of money for it. First Jock and I worked and made some, and then everybody gave money. Mr. Digby is going to give all that you need after we find out how much there is altogether. Even Aunt Hannah is going to give some because she loves Jesus now, and the Camps and everybody. I found Mr. Digby's wallet and got a reward. He is very nice. I think Mr. Digby and Aunt Hannah are taking care of all the business about the hospital, because I don't know how. Goodbye for now.

Love,

Biddy

Aunt Hannah and Mr. Digby did have some business to take care of about the hospital, and they sent many letters to

China and to London. They had long talks together about how it would be built, and where and when, and decided that Mr. Digby would go to China to take care of details!

Biddy wished that she could go too. She got homesick when she thought of China. She thought how nice it would be if she could see the hospital when it was all built. But when she thought of all her friends in England, and of all the people there who still didn't know about Jesus, she knew it was best for her to stay where she was.

One day a very special letter came for her. It was from Mommy. "Dear Biddy," it said. "We have a surprise for you. Soon you will have a little sister or brother. Since there is so much sickness in China, the new baby should stay somewhere else for a while. The rest is a secret!"

Biddy was so curious and so excited that she could hardly sit still to eat her meals. "Do you know the secret, Aunt Hannah?" she asked at lunchtime. "What is Mommy's secret?"

"Oh, you can't tell secrets!" said Aunt Hannah with a smile, and Biddy thought that she must know, but she wouldn't tell.

Aunt Hannah did tell Biddy how much money had been saved for the hospital. First they added up the money that Biddy had saved in her box—and discovered the check from Maria. Then they added up what was in the bank, and they found that there was over two hundred dollars.

"Froggy has been sold for nine hundred dollars," said Aunt Hannah, "and I have sold my jewelry for five hundred dollars. That makes one thousand and six hundred dollars for the hospital, and Mr. Digby will give the rest. I think there's going to be a fine, large hospital in China."

Biddy waited impatiently for some clue to her mother's secret, but nothing came—no more letters, no hints from Aunt Hannah. Days and weeks went by. Biddy had to begin lessons in the fall, and Jock had to go back to Scotland to boarding school. Things seemed to be very quiet.

Then one day, about two months after her mother's letter had come, Biddy saw a taxi come up in front of the house. She watched to see who would get out. When she saw who it was, she ran outside and all the way down the steps and out to the car, because there were Amah and her own mother. Mommy handed a bundle of white blanket to Amah and reached out to take Biddy in her arms and give her a big hug!

"Mommy! Mommy! You came all the way to England to see me!"

"Yes, I did, Biddy. I've missed you very much. Would you like to see your brother?"

Amah stooped down so that Biddy could look in at the little face in the blanket. "I hope he's like Jock," said Biddy. "I mean, when he grows up."

Biddy took one hand of her mother's and one of Amah's and together they went into the house.

"This is the best surprise of all," said Biddy. "I wish Daddy could have come."

"Daddy is building the hospital that you helped to buy," said her mother. "And of course, the people in China are still sick. He has to take care of them."

"It was really the little green frog that got everything started," said Biddy. "Amah, do you feel bad because I sold the frog?"

"Oh, no," said Amah. "If the frog helps to let people know about Jesus, then I am glad to have you sell him. God has used the little green frog to bring us much happiness."